Disney · PIXAR
Storybook
Collection

This edition published by Parragon Books Ltd in 2014

Parragon Books Ltd
Chartist House
15–17 Trim Street
Bath BA1 1HA, UK
www.parragon.com

ISBN 978-1-4723-5696-3

Printed in China

Disney · PIXAR
Storybook
Collection

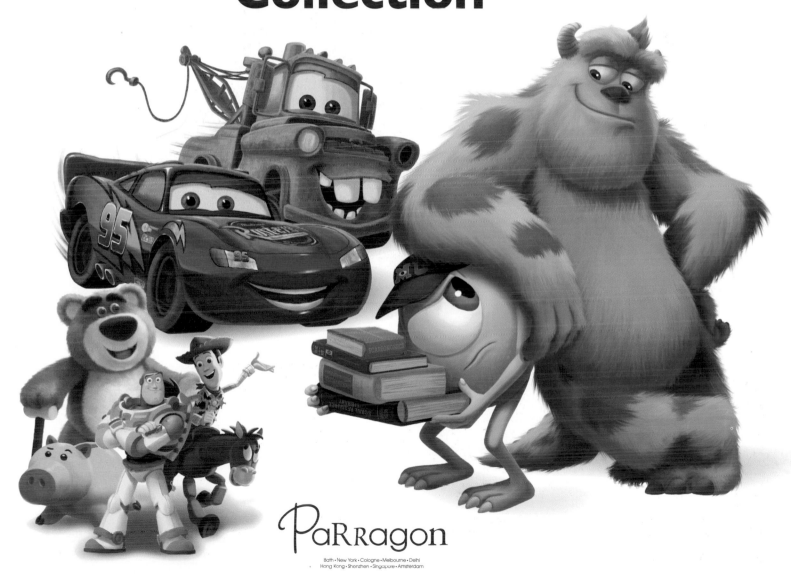

PaRragon

Bath · New York · Cologne · Melbourne · Delhi
Hong Kong · Shenzhen · Singapore · Amsterdam

Contents

Lightning McQueen was taking part in the biggest race of the season – the Dinoco 400. The current champion, The King, and Lightning's racing rival, Chick Hicks, were also racing. This was to be The King's last ever race, which meant that the lucrative Dinoco sponsorship was up for grabs.

When Lightning pulled into the pits, he filled up with petrol but ignored his crew's advice to change tyres. He increased his lead, but it was a risky strategy.

During the last lap his back tyres blew out. Chick and The King drew level with him just as he limped across the finishing line.

It was too close to call!

While Lightning waited for the race results, he posed for the reporters, pushing his pit crew aside.

"Ka-chow! I'm a one-man show!" Furious, his pit crew quit on the spot.

Then the announcement came. "Ladies and gentlemen, for the first time in Piston Cup history, we have a three-way tie!"

A tie-breaker race would be held in California in one week's time.

Lightning ordered his lorry, Mack, to drive through the night to California.
He promised Mack that he would stay up with him, but he soon fell asleep.
Many hours later, a gang of cars pulled alongside the exhausted lorry and
began bumping him for a laugh. Mack swerved dangerously and Lightning,
still sleeping, rolled out of the trailer onto the road.

Lightning woke up among oncoming traffic! He thought he saw Mack pull off the road and he quickly followed. Unfortunately, it turned out that it wasn't Mack he had followed ... Lightning was lost!

Feeling panicked, Lightning tore off up the main street of a small town, destroying everything in his path. He ended up dangling helplessly between two telegraph poles!

"Boy, you're in a heap of trouble," said the Sheriff.

The next morning, Lightning woke up to see a cheery tow truck grinning at him from the gates of a car pound.

"Hi, there! My name's Mater," he said. "Welcome to Radiator Springs!"

At that moment, the Sheriff arrived to escort Lightning to court. The judge, Doc Hudson, wanted to kick Lightning out of town, but Sally, the lawyer, had a better idea; Lightning couldn't leave until he had repaired the town's damaged road.

Reluctantly, Lightning set to work pulling Bessie, the enormous road-surfacing machine. When he heard a radio report that Chick was already in California practising for the tie-breaker race, he pulled Bessie as hard and fast as he could.

A couple of hours later, Lightning announced that the road was finished … but it was a total mess. "Now it matches the rest of the town," sneered Lightning.

Doc was furious. He decided to settle matters with a race.

"If you win, you go and I fix the road. If I win, you do the road my way,"
he said.

Out at the dirt track, Lightning took a quick lead, but he made a mistake
on a tricky bend and wiped out!

Mater hauled Lightning out of the ditch and he was sent back to work. By
the next morning, Radiator Springs had a patch of beautifully surfaced road.

Lightning was tired and filthy, but the townsfolk thanked him.

That night, Mater took Lightning tractor-tipping. Mater sneaked up on a sleeping tractor and honked. The startled tractor woke up and fell over! When it was Lightning's turn, he revved his engine so loudly, all the tractors keeled over at the same time. Mater and Lightning could not stop laughing.

As they returned to the motel, Mater showed off his amazing backwards-driving tricks. Lightning was impressed.

"Maybe I'll use it in my big race," Lightning said thoughtfully.

When Lightning told Mater that winning the race meant getting a new sponsor with private helicopters, Mater got excited. He asked if he could ride in a helicopter some day. Lightning agreed casually.

Sally had overheard Lightning and Mater's conversation. "Did you mean it?" she asked. "You know, Mater trusts you."

The next morning, Lightning saw three Piston Cups in Doc's shop!
He was amazed – Doc Hudson was a racing legend!

Doc was furious when he found Lightning in his shop.

"All I see is a bunch of empty cups," Doc said, pushing Lightning out
and slamming the door.

Lightning rushed over to Flo's Café to tell everyone that Doc was a famous race car. But no one believed him. While the other cars were laughing, Sally filled Lightning's tank. Sheriff was worried that Lightning would leave, but Sally surprised everyone – including Lightning.

"I trust him," she said. "Let's go for a drive."

The two cars zoomed up a mountain road and Lightning realized that he was racing, just for fun, for the first time. He also noticed how beautiful the scenery and Sally were.

Sally told Lightning how she had been a lawyer in L.A., but she hadn't been happy. One day, she just drove and drove until she reached Radiator Springs.

"I fell in love with this," Sally continued. Far below lay a gorgeous valley surrounded by copper-coloured mountains. In the distance, Lightning saw cars speeding past on the Interstate.

"They don't even know what they're missing," he murmured.

Later that day, Lightning saw Doc roaring round the dirt racetrack.
"You're amazing!" Lightning told the old pro, but Doc raced off.
Lightning followed Doc to his office.

"How could you quit at the top of your game?" Lightning asked.

Doc showed Lightning a newspaper article about a crash he had
been in. After he was repaired, Doc wanted to return to racing. But he
had been replaced – by a rookie.

The next morning, the road was finished, but where was Lightning?
Had he left for California? Everyone felt sad.

Just then, Lightning rolled up. He hadn't left!

"I knew you wouldn't go without saying goodbye!" Mater exclaimed.

Lightning explained that he had a few things to do before leaving. He spent
the rest of the day using every shop in town. He got new tyres, a new paint job
and fuel from Fillmore. Lightning liked helping the town's small businesses …

... and Lightning liked teaming up with his new friends!

"Is it getting dark out?" he called loudly when Sally drove up. Suddenly, Radiator Springs lit up in glowing neon colours and music played. It was time to cruise!

As the townsfolk drove together in pairs, a helicopter searchlight swept over them.

"We have found Lightning McQueen!" boomed a voice from a loudspeaker.

News vans swarmed into town. Reporters surrounded Lightning, shouting questions. He couldn't see Sally or reach his friends.

Lightning's agent wanted Lightning to leave Radiator Springs straight away. Lightning and Sally gazed at each other. Neither of them knew what to say.

"Good luck in California," Sally said at last. "I hope you find what you're looking for."

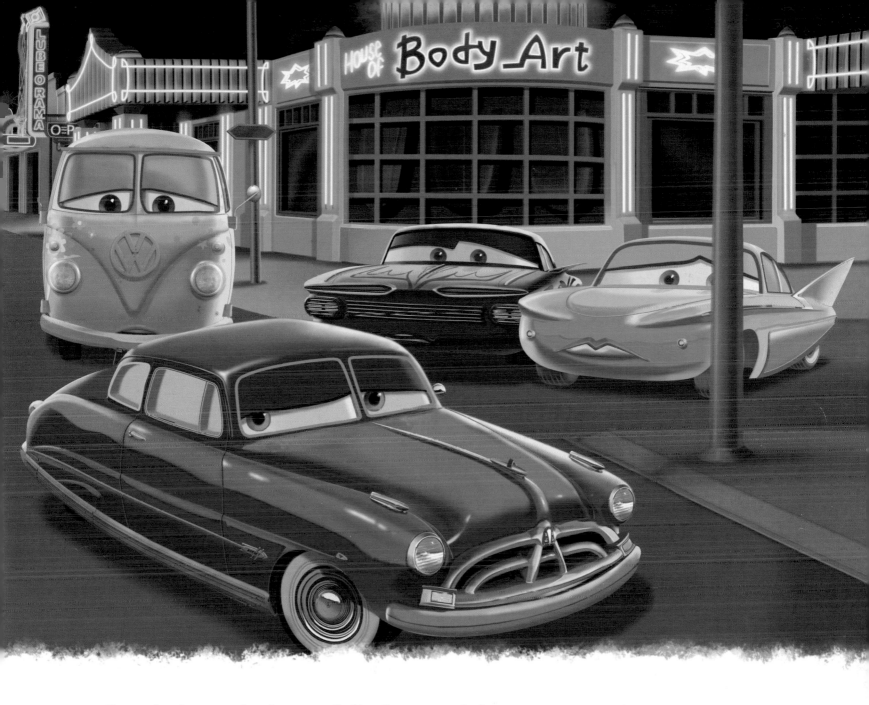

Once Lightning had gone, Sally discovered that it was Doc who gave away Lightning's location.

"It's best for everyone, Sally," Doc explained.

Sally was shocked. "Or best for you?"

In a packed stadium in California, the tie-breaker race for the Piston Cup started. But Lightning couldn't concentrate. He kept remembering his friends in Radiator Springs. Somehow, winning no longer seemed that important to Lightning.

Just then, Doc's voice came over the radio: "I didn't come all this way to see you quit."

Inspired by his friends – his new pit crew – Lightning raced round the track, closing the gap. Chick tried his usual dirty tricks, but Lightning remembered what his friends had taught him.

Lightning was in the lead! Chick and The King were fighting for second place. Suddenly, Chick rammed the veteran race car. The King hit a wall and flipped.

When Lightning saw The King's crumpled body, he remembered Doc's final crash. Lightning screeched to a stop – inches from the finish line.

As Chick won the race, Lightning drove over to The King. He thought the veteran should finish his last race. As he pushed The King over the finish line, the crowd erupted in cheers.

Chick won the Piston Cup, but Lightning was the hero of the race!

Tex, Dinoco's owner, asked Lightning, "How would you like to be the new face of Dinoco?"

Lightning politely refused, deciding to stay loyal to his original sponsor.

A little later, back in Radiator Springs, Lightning found Sally. They heard someone wildly yelling, "Wooo-hoo!"

It was Mater, taking his first helicopter ride! Sally smiled. Lightning had remembered his promise.

She revved her engine before speeding off down the mountain, with Lightning close behind. It looked as if the rookie race car had found his new home.

When Mike Wazowski was six years old, he went on a field trip to Monsters, Inc. He sneaked inside a child's bedroom and saw a Scarer at work. That one amazing moment made Mike realize he wanted to be a Scarer himself when he grew up!

The years passed and finally Mike was old enough to attend the School of Scaring at Monsters University. Mike arrived on campus filled with excitement. His childhood dream was about to start coming true!

One of Mike's classmates was a huge monster named Sulley. He belonged to the Roar Omega Roar fraternity. Sulley and the RORs made fun of Mike. They thought he was too small and funny looking to be a Scarer.

Mike was determined to study hard and ace his final exam. Meanwhile, all Sulley did was mess around. He thought that being big and having a loud roar were enough to make him the best Scarer.

During the final exam, Mike and Sulley got into a roaring face-off. They accidentally broke Dean Hardscrabble's prized scream can. Hardscrabble continued giving Mike and Sulley their exam. Then she decided that neither of them would be staying in the Scaring Programme and Sulley had to leave the Roar Omega Roar fraternity!

Winning the annual Scare Games was Mike and Sulley's only way of getting back into the Scaring Programme. To compete in the games, they had to join a fraternity. They joined the least scary group on campus: Oozma Kappa. The members of OK were Don, Squishy, Art and Terri and Terry.

Mike wasn't happy about working with Sulley – but he had no choice.

The first Scare Games event was the Toxicity Challenge. The teams had to get from one end of a sewer tunnel to the other while avoiding stinging glow urchins. The second the race started, Mike and Sulley took off and left the rest of the OKs behind. The entire team ended up coming in last. Oozma Kappa was out!

Then, suddenly, one of the winning teams was disqualified for cheating. The OKs were back in!

The next day, the OKs showed Mike some of their talents, but Mike already had a plan. "From now on we are of one mind … *my* mind," he said.

Sulley rolled his eyes. "You tell them what to do, but not me. Later coach," he muttered.

The second event, Avoid the Parent,
took place in the library. The teams
had to capture their flag without
getting caught by the librarian! Even
though Sulley was no help to the team
at all, the OKs managed to take fourth
place. Squishy had grabbed the flag
and made it out of the library without
anyone noticing!

Just as the OKs were starting to feel confident, the RORs made fun of them.
They told the OKs they'd never be real Scarers.

Mike decided to take everyone to Monsters, Inc. They sneaked up onto the
roof and looked down onto a scare floor. They saw that Scarers came in all
shapes and sizes. Everyone was inspired.

Mike and Sulley both admitted that they had been behaving badly.
They agreed they needed to start working together.

The following morning, Mike and Sulley bounded out of bed.
They couldn't wait to begin training for the next Scare Games event!
They packed up their gear, met up with the other OKs and headed off
to campus.

Mike worked on getting the team in tip-top shape. He taught them how to sneak into a bedroom, how to drop to the floor and how to dodge teenagers. In between drills, Mike got them to run on the spot and practise their 'scary feet'.

The Oozma Kappas' training paid off. They passed the Don't Scare the Teen event and moved to the next round! Mike helped them to practise for the Hide and Sneak event. The OKs were so well prepared, they came in second.

They were heading to the finals!

Later, Sulley ran into Dean Hardscrabble.

"Tomorrow each of you must prove that you are undeniably scary and I know one of you is not," she said.

Sulley knew that she meant Mike. He didn't want to believe her, but he couldn't help but wonder if she was right.

The RORs and the OKs were going head-to-head in the final Scare Games event. Each competitor had to perform a scare in a simulator.

Mike was the last member of the OKs to perform his scare. He entered the room, sneaked up to the bed, leaped up and roared! The robot child sat bolt upright and screamed.

Mike's scare had given the OKs the highest score. They had won the Scare Games! Don, Squishy, Art, Terri and Terry and Sulley all surrounded Mike and lifted him on their shoulders. The entire amphitheatre burst into cheers and applause.

"We're in the Scaring Programme!" Sulley cried.

But the moment didn't last long. Mike soon discovered that Sulley had rigged the controls on the simulator. Mike's difficulty level had been switched to 'easy'. He couldn't believe it!

"Well, what was I supposed to do?" Sulley blurted out. "Let the whole team fail because you don't have it?"

Mike was angry. He stormed off and stole a key to the Door Tech Lab, where students learned how to build doors to the human world. He put a scream can in place, powered up a door – and opened it! Alarms went off all over campus, sending Hardscrabble and her security guards racing to the lab.

Mike found himself in the wardrobe of a child's room. He crept out towards the sleeping child and ... **ROARED!**

The youngster sat up and smiled. "You look funny," she said.

Mike couldn't believe it. Suddenly, he realized he wasn't in a child's bedroom. He turned to look and saw that he was in a cabin full of kids!

Meanwhile, Sulley rushed to the lab. He slipped past security, ran through the door and went off to rescue Mike. He found him beside a lake in the camp grounds.

"I thought I could show everybody that Mike Wazowski is something special. But I'm just not," said Mike.

Sulley told Mike he wasn't much different. He had messed things up his entire life. "I'll never know how you feel, but you're not the only 'failure' here," he said.

Mike and Sulley returned to the cabin, but the door back to Monsters University had been powered down. They were trapped! A group of adults was now quickly approaching.

"If we really scare them, we could generate enough scream to power the door from this side," said Mike.

As the adults entered the cabin, Mike and Sulley set up their big scare. Then, on Mike's cue, Sulley loomed over the adults and **ROARED!**

The adults screamed and ran for their lives. Back in the Door Tech Lab, the door's scream can filled to the brim! Hardscrabble watched in disbelief as the door exploded and Mike and Sulley blasted into the room.

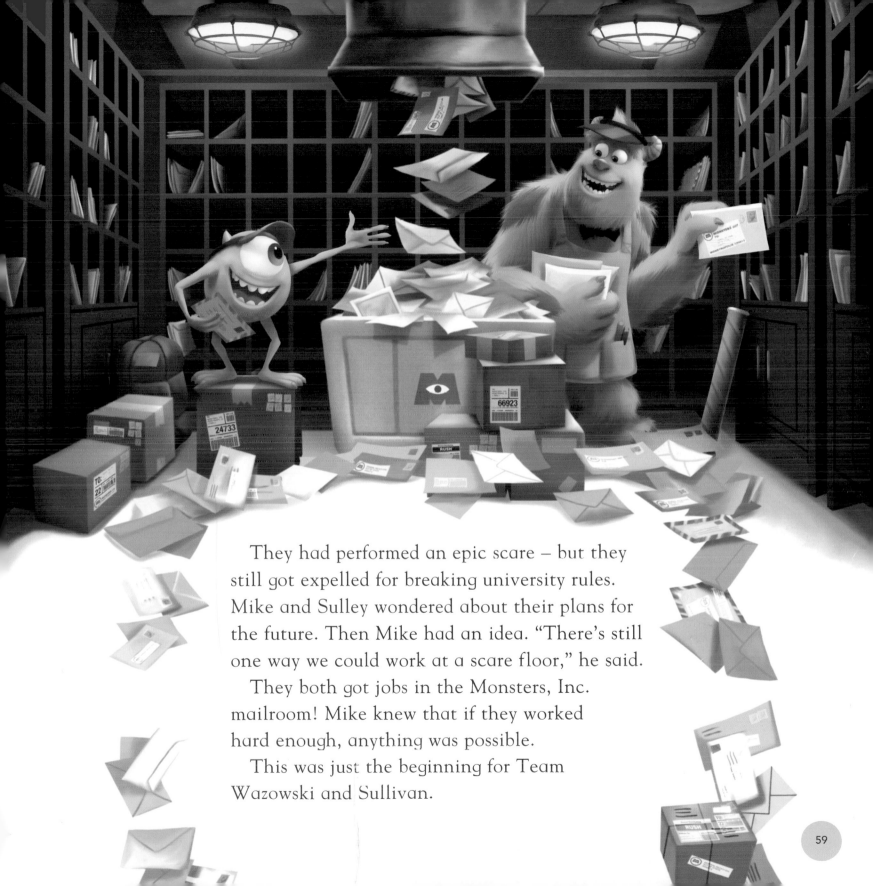

They had performed an epic scare – but they still got expelled for breaking university rules. Mike and Sulley wondered about their plans for the future. Then Mike had an idea. "There's still one way we could work at a scare floor," he said.

They both got jobs in the Monsters, Inc. mailroom! Mike knew that if they worked hard enough, anything was possible.

This was just the beginning for Team Wazowski and Sullivan.

Andy loved his toys and they loved him. Sheriff Woody, Buzz Lightyear, Jessie the cowgirl, Rex, Hamm and all the rest were happiest when they were off on one of Andy's wildly imaginative adventures. It didn't matter whether Andy pretended the toys had X-ray vision or superhuman strength, or whether he made them villains or heroes. The toys all agreed: simply being played with by a kid – by Andy – was the best feeling in the world.

But as Andy grew into a teenager, he played with the toys less and less.
By the time he was preparing for college, the toys were very worried.
What would happen to them? Woody tried to reassure everyone.
Andy would just tuck them all in the attic for safekeeping, he explained.

Andy's mum had another idea, however. She suggested that Andy donate
his old toys to a daycare centre.

"No one's going to want those," he told her. "They're junk."

The toys were shocked. Then Andy opened the toy box, scooped up Rex,
Hamm, Slinky and Mr and Mrs Potato Head – and dumped them into a rubbish
bag! He paused for a moment, looking at his two favourites, Buzz and Woody.
Then, he dropped Woody into a box marked 'College' – and Buzz went into
the rubbish bag, too!

At first, the toys thought they were headed for the bin. But in fact, Andy planned to put the bag in the attic. Then Andy's mum made a terrible mistake. She assumed the bag was rubbish and dumped it at the kerb.

Frantic, Woody climbed out the window to help his friends. He was still looking for them when the bin lorry arrived. He watched in horror as the bin man hurled the bags into the back of the lorry and crushed the entire load with the lorry's compactor!

Then Woody noticed an upside-down recycling bin moving across Andy's driveway. His friends had escaped!

Inside the garage, the toys were hurt and confused. What would they do now that Andy had thrown them away?

Jessie had an idea: go to the daycare centre! She convinced everyone to climb inside the box of old toys that Mum planned to donate.

Woody followed his friends into the box. He tried to explain about the rubbish bag mix-up, but the toys didn't believe him.

SLAM! Suddenly, Andy's mum shut the hatchback, got in and started driving.

Woody had been hoping to lead everyone back to Andy, but Jessie convinced the group that wouldn't work. Didn't Woody understand that Andy didn't want them anymore?

Soon the receptionist at Sunnyside Daycare was carrying the box of toys down to the daycare centre's Butterfly Room.

While the children were playing, Andy's toys couldn't contain their excitement and spilled out onto the floor. The daycare toys welcomed them with open arms.

Friendliest of all was a big, pink bear who smelled like strawberries. "Welcome to Sunnyside!" he called warmly. "I'm Lots-o'-Huggin' Bear! But, please, call me Lotso!"

"Mr Lotso," asked Rex. "Do toys here get played with every day?"

"All day long," Lotso answered. "When the kids get old, new ones come in. No owners means no heartbreak."

To the toys, daycare was sounding better and better!

Lotso and a doll named Big Baby led the toys on a tour of Sunnyside before escorting them to their new home at Sunnyside: the Caterpillar Room.

Woody begged his friends not to stay. They belonged at Andy's house.

But Jessie and the others disagreed. "We can have a new life here, Woody," the cowgirl argued.

Woody could see his friends' minds were made up. Feeling sad and conflicted, he said goodbye.

He clambered onto the roof and used an old kite to propel himself over the daycare centre's walls. When he crash-landed a little while later, he was bruised, hatless and dangling by his pull-string from a tree branch.

The receptionist's daughter, Bonnie, ran over to the dangling cowboy and shoved him into her rucksack. Then she took him home.

Inside the Caterpillar Room, Andy's toys waited excitedly as footsteps thundered towards them. Suddenly, a crowd of toddlers burst into the room. They tangled Slinky's coil, dipped Jessie's hair in paint and covered Hamm with glitter and glue.

One of the toddlers threw Buzz onto a windowsill. He could see into the Butterfly Room … where a group of four- and five-year-olds were playing gently with Lotso and the other daycare toys.

Buzz wondered: why had Andy's toys been put in the Caterpillar Room? The toddlers' play was too rough!

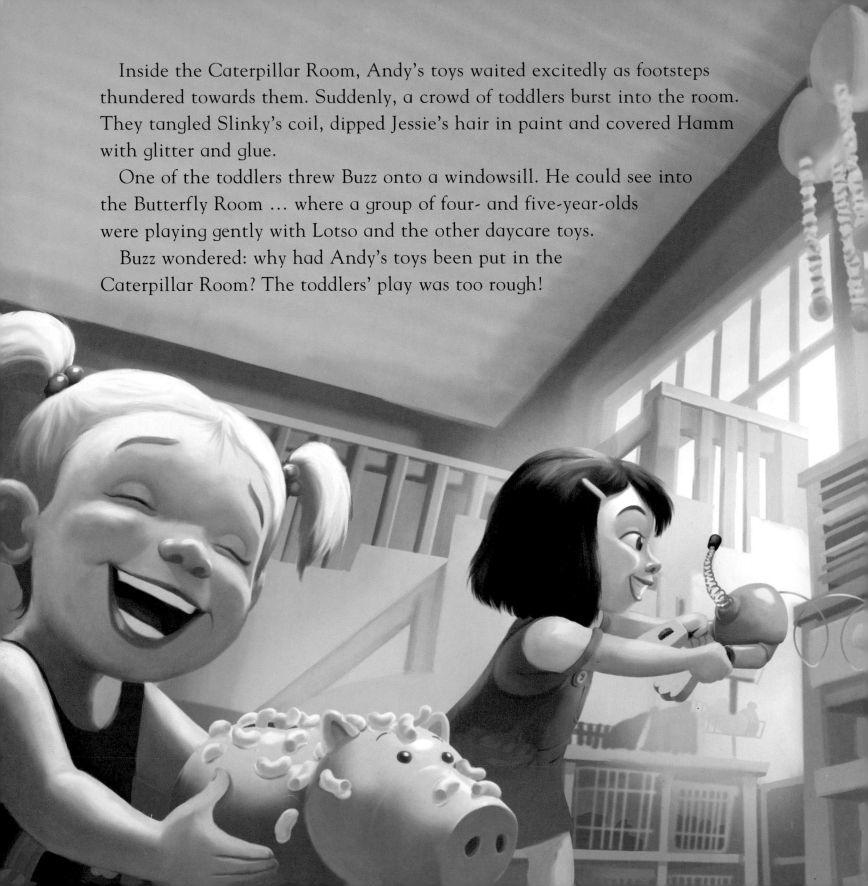

After the children went home, the toys tried to put themselves back together.
"I'll go talk to Lotso about moving us to the other room," said Buzz.

Then they discovered all the doors and windows were locked. Finally, Buzz
escaped through an open window above the door.

While he was gone, Mrs Potato Head started to see strange images, coming
to her through the eye she'd lost back at Andy's house.

"Andy's looking in the attic," she said. "Why is he so upset?" She gasped.
"I think he did mean to put us in the attic!"

Now that the toys realized their mistake, they knew they had to go home!

Buzz found some of the Sunnyside toys inside a vending machine. He overheard them talking – and learned that these toys knew how dangerous the Caterpillar Room was. Andy's toys had been sent there on purpose! Buzz tried to go and warn his friends, but he was captured.

When Lotso arrived, he was as friendly as ever. He even granted Buzz's request to be transferred to the Butterfly Room – on the condition that Buzz's friends stay behind.

"I can't accept," said Buzz. "We're a family. We stay together."

Suddenly, Lotso's attitude changed. With a cruel smile, he called for the Buzz Lightyear Instruction Manual. Then he ordered his gang to reset Buzz's switch to 'Demo Mode'.

When Lotso arrived in the Caterpillar Room, Andy's toys begged to leave.

"Here's the thing," the bear said, grinning nastily. "You ain't leaving Sunnyside." He wanted Andy's toys to stay with the littlest kids. Somebody had to endure their rough play and it wasn't going to be Lotso's gang!

Then, suddenly, Buzz appeared and accused his old friends of being 'minions of Zurg'!

Jessie and the others were shocked. What had happened to Buzz?

Lotso's gang herded Andy's toys into the room's wire cubbies. When Mr Potato Head fought back, Big Baby made him stay overnight in a covered sandbox out in the playground.

Lotso chuckled and left, leaving the captives under Buzz's stern guard. The happy daycare had turned into a grim prison!

Meanwhile, at Bonnie's house, Woody was actually having fun. The little girl had a great imagination and her toys were very kind.

But then Woody discovered he was just a few streets from Andy's house!

"If you guys ever get to Sunnyside Daycare," said Woody, waving goodbye, "tell them Woody made it home."

The toys gasped. They knew all about Sunnyside. Long ago, explained a toy clown called Chuckles, he, Lotso and Big Baby had belonged to a girl named Daisy. One day, the toys had been left behind on a trip. Lotso led them home, but Daisy already had a new pink bear. Heartbroken, Lotso ripped off the pendant with Daisy's name on it that Big Baby always wore. Eventually, the trio came to Sunnyside – where Lotso became the daycare centre's bitter tyrant. Chuckles would have perished, except that Bonnie rescued him after he was broken.

While Woody wanted to get home to Andy, he knew he couldn't leave his friends in Lotso's clutches. The next day, he hitched a ride to Sunnyside in Bonnie's rucksack.

The cowboy found his pals and they made a plan to break out. That night, Woody and Slinky surprised the toy monkey who sat by the security monitors, and grabbed the daycare keys. Mr Potato Head distracted Big Baby while the others captured Buzz. Meanwhile, Barbie forced Ken to tell her about Buzz's instruction manual. She and the other toys attempted to reset Buzz's switch – but now Buzz only spoke Spanish!

Despite the setbacks, everyone made it to the rubbish chute in the playground.

Woody and the rest of
the toys climbed into
the rubbish chute
and slid down
one by one.

At the
bottom, Slinky
formed a bridge
between the chute and
the lid of the nearby
bin so his friends
could walk across
to freedom.

But suddenly, Lotso appeared. "Why don't you come back and join our family again?" he asked the toys.

"You're a liar and a bully and I'd rather rot in this bin than join any family of yours!" Jessie replied.

Lotso scowled. "I didn't throw you away," he replied. "Your kid did. There isn't one kid who ever loved a toy, really."

"What about Daisy?" Woody asked suddenly. "She lost you. By accident. She loved you!" He threw down the old pendant that Chuckles had given him.

"She never loved me!" Lotso exploded angrily. "She left me!"

Big Baby's eyes filled with tears as he thought about Daisy.

"You want your Mummy back? She never loved you!" Lotso shouted and gave Big Baby a shove.

Big Baby had had enough. He hoisted Lotso into the air – and threw him into a big rubbish bin!

The daycare toys cheered. Things would be different at Sunnyside from now on.

"Come on! Hurry!" cried Woody, starting across the lid. He could hear a rubbish lorry rumbling towards them!

The toys followed and climbed to safety on a wall.

Then Woody saw an Alien caught in between the bin lids. The cowboy ran back, but Lotso reached up and yanked Woody inside! The rest of Andy's toys jumped onto the lid and tried to pry it open, but the rubbish lorry lifted the container and tilted it upside down. Soon all the toys fell into the back of the rubbish lorry.

The lorry rumbled forwards, then lurched to a stop. More rubbish rained down on them and a TV landed on top of Buzz. Incredibly, the blow turned him back into his old self!

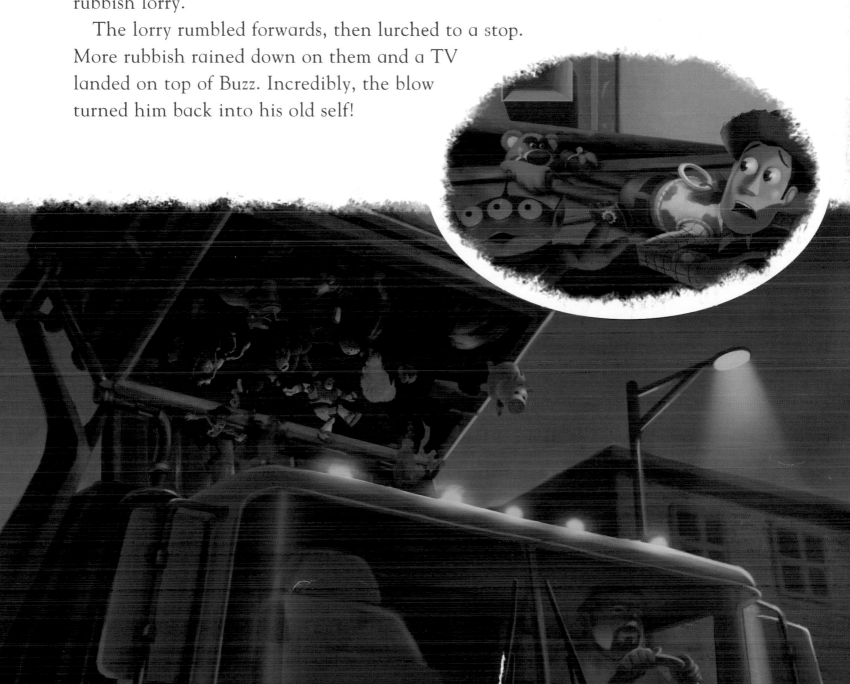

Soon the lorry arrived at the Tri-County Landfill and dumped its load.

"The claaaaw!" shouted the Aliens excitedly as they toddled off towards a crane in the distance.

Woody tried to go after them, but was cut off by a huge bulldozer. Rumbling, it pushed him and his friends towards an open pit.

The toys fell onto a conveyor belt that led to a shredder. But they soon discovered another conveyor belt above them that was magnetic. They grabbed onto whatever metal rubbish they could find and were lifted to safety.

Suddenly, they heard a cry for help. Lotso was trapped! Woody and Buzz dropped down and used a golf club to free him. The shredder was just inches away!

Woody grabbed Lotso's paw, the golf club flew towards the magnet and all three were lifted to safety. Next they dropped down to their friends, who were on another conveyor belt far below.

They thought they saw daylight at the end of this belt – but suddenly realized it was actually an incinerator!

Lotso managed to find the Emergency Stop Button that could save them all, but instead of pushing it, he hesitated. Then a cruel smirk came across his face and he ran off.

Woody and his friends tumbled towards the fire, determined to face it the best way they knew how: together.

Then, suddenly, a large shadow passed over them. A giant crane lowered its jaws and scooped the toys up and away from the scorching fire. Inside the crane's cab, the Aliens steered their friends over the landfill and dropped them gently to the ground.

Now the toys had to get Woody home before Andy left for college. Luckily, they spotted their neighbourhood rubbish man nearby, just climbing into his lorry. The toys hurried forwards, ready to hitch a ride home.

Lotso found his way onto a different lorry. But he wouldn't be hopping off anytime soon – he had been tied to the front of it!

Woody and the gang arrived home as Andy was loading up the car. They had made it just in time!

Woody headed for a box marked 'College', while the others climbed into an 'Attic' box. Before they separated, Woody and Buzz shook hands.

"You know where to find us, Cowboy," Buzz said finally.

Inside the 'College' box, Woody looked at a photo of Andy with all his toys. The cowboy knew that – no matter where any of them went – they would always carry the memories of their time together.

Suddenly, Woody had an idea. He jumped out of the box, hastily wrote something on a sticky note, and placed it on the attic box.

Attic

When Andy arrived to grab the last boxes, he read the note. Then he opened
the attic box and got a wonderful surprise – his toys hadn't been thrown away,
after all!

"Hey, Mum," he shouted. "Do you really think I should donate these?"

"It's up to you," she called back.

A little while later, Andy pulled up to Bonnie's house.

"Someone told me you're really good with toys," Andy said to the
little girl.

As Andy introduced his toys to Bonnie, he was startled to find Woody in the
box. He wasn't supposed to be there!

"My cowboy!" Bonnie cried happily.

Though it was hard for him, Andy let Woody stay with
Bonnie, too. From the hug she gave the cowboy, Andy
could see that she already loved him.

Back in the car, Andy took one last look at a smiling Bonnie surrounded by his toys.

"Thanks, guys," he said quietly before pulling away.

Bonnie went inside for lunch and the toys watched Andy disappear down the street.

"So long, partner," said Woody.

Buzz and the others gathered round him. Their life with Andy was ending, but their adventures with Bonnie had only just begun.

Marlin was a clownfish, but that didn't mean he had to find life funny.

Marlin had lost his wife and more than four hundred eggs in a ruthless barracuda attack. Only one egg had survived, but he had one damaged fin.

"I promise I will never let anything happen to you … Nemo," Marlin said.

After Nemo was born, Marlin wouldn't let him out of his sight. Marlin was so protective, he didn't even like him going beyond their sea anemone home. But, on Nemo's first day of school, Nemo was ready for adventure!

"Wake up, wake up! C'mon!" Nemo exclaimed, swimming circles around his sleeping father.

Before they set off for school, Marlin asked sternly, "What's the one thing we have to remember about the ocean?"

"It's not safe," Nemo sighed.

As they swam to school together, Marlin kept reminding Nemo to hold his fin.

Nemo had made some new friends from his class and they sneaked off together, daring each other to swim out into the open sea. Nemo was nervous and didn't venture very far, but it was way too far for Marlin, who was hovering nearby.

Nemo wanted to prove his dad wrong.
He swam towards a passing boat. Suddenly, a
diver appeared…. "Daddy! Help me!" Nemo
screamed as he caught sight of his reflection in
the diver's mask.

In a flash, the diver had scooped Nemo up
in a net. Marlin raced to the surface as the
divers sped away.

There was nothing he could do to save his
precious son. Their boat had sped off so quickly
that a diver's mask had fallen overboard.

Marlin rushed to a busy underwater road to get help.

"Has anybody seen a boat?" he cried.

A beautiful blue tang named Dory told him that she had seen a boat! "Follow me!" she said.

However, Dory had a very bad memory. One minute later, she couldn't even remember why Marlin was following her!

"Will you quit it?" she asked.

Confused, Marlin turned to swim away. Only to come face to face with …

... a huge shark!

He was called Bruce and he was trying to be a vegetarian. He befriended Dory and Marlin and wanted them to meet his like-minded buddies, so they could prove their motto: "Fish are friends, not food!"

Dory, who was as enthusiastic as she was forgetful, thought it was a wonderful idea. Terrified Marlin did not.

The 'self-help' sharks held their meetings in a wrecked submarine.
"It has been three weeks since my last fish," Bruce told his friends proudly.
Always eager, Dory joined in. "I don't think I've ever eaten a fish."
Just then, Marlin spotted the diver's mask! Dory wanted to show it
to the sharks but Marlin didn't. As they tussled, Dory bumped her nose and it
bled a little. Bruce got a sudden craving for a fish dinner!
As Dory and Marlin tried to escape, something exploded!

Meanwhile, Nemo found himself in a dentist's fish tank in Sydney. He soon discovered how small the tank was when he crashed into the side.

A group of fish soon came out of hiding. Bubbles, Peach, Jacques, Bloat, Deb and Gurgle were thrilled to meet a fish from the open sea.

Later, Nemo learned that he was to be a present for the dentist's niece, Darla.

"She's a fish-killer," whispered Peach, the starfish.

That night, a ceremony was held to make Nemo an official member of their group. All Nemo had to do was swim through the **RING OF FIRE!**

It sounded scary, but it was really just a stream of bubbles. Nemo bravely swam through the bubbles and into the gang's hearts.

Afterwards Gill, the leader of the tank, announced, "From this moment on, you will now be known as 'Shark Bait'." Next, he revealed his plan to escape from the tank....

Back in the ocean, Dory had dropped the mask into a deep trench! She and Marlin swam after it and ran into an anglerfish.

Suddenly, Dory remembered she could read!

"P. Sherman, 42 Wallaby Way, Sydney," said Dory.

Thinking quickly, Marlin trapped the anglerfish inside the mask. The pair were so excited – they knew where to find Nemo!

Marlin told Dory he was going to Sydney alone.
"You mean you don't like me?" Dory asked.

A school of moonfish rushed over and were angry
with Marlin for upsetting Dory. They refused
to help Marlin but, when he turned
his back, they told Dory how to
get to Sydney. "Follow the East
Australian Current," they said.

Then, they gave her a warning.
"When you come to a trench, swim
through it, not over it."

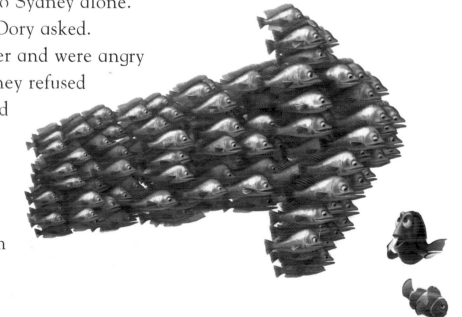

When they finally got to the trench, however, Marlin insisted that
swimming over it would be much safer. Soon they were surrounded by stinging
jellyfish! Dory thought it was fun to bounce on top of them! They had found
a safe way through – but they were tired and had been stung by the jellyfish.
They needed help.

Luckily, some sea turtles arrived and rescued Marlin and Dory. Their run-in with the jellyfish had left them in bad shape.

"Takin' on the jellies – awesome!" exclaimed Crush, a surfer turtle.

Marlin watched as Crush encouraged his children to be adventurous. He thought it taught them important lessons. Watching Crush's kids made Marlin wonder if he had been too protective of Nemo.

Meanwhile, tales of Marlin's adventures were spreading far and wide. Nigel, a friendly pelican who knew the Tank Gang, eventually heard the stories and rushed to tell Nemo the incredible news.

Nemo was amazed. He had always thought his dad was a bit of a scaredy-fish. The thought that he was battling his way to Sydney filled the little fish with pride.

Nemo was inspired by his dad's bravery
and he was determined to escape. To his
friends' surprise, Nemo darted into the
filter and successfully jammed it!
Everyone cheered!

Very soon, the Tank Gang was swimming
in slimy, green water. They couldn't have been
happier! Dr Sherman was going to have to take
them out and clean the tank before Darla arrived.

Back in the ocean, Marlin and Dory said goodbye to the turtles, but soon found themselves inside the mouth of a massive whale.

"It's okay, I speak Whale," Dory assured Marlin. "He either said we should move to the back of his throat, or he wants a root beer float," she translated.

It turned out the whale was only giving the two brave little fish a lift. They were soon squirted out of the whale's blow-hole, right into Sydney Harbour!

They nearly ended up as breakfast for some hungry
seagulls, but eventually they escaped … and landed
on the dock.

Luckily, Nigel rushed to their rescue.

"Hop inside my mouth if you want to live,"
he whispered.

Nigel snatched them up, filled his
beak with some water and took off.
The hungry seagulls followed, but Nigel
played a trick on them and the seagulls
flew right into a boat's sail!

Inside, the dentist had cleaned the tank water with a fancy new automated cleaner – while the fish were still in the tank!

The escape plan was ruined.

Nemo was lifted out of the tank and plopped into a bag. Darla had arrived. Nemo had one last chance – he played dead, hoping that he would get flushed down the toilet and out into the ocean.

Nigel stumbled through the window with Marlin and Dory and saw Nemo floating upside down in the plastic bag. The dentist quickly shooed Nigel away, but in the commotion he dropped Nemo. The bag burst open.

"I get a fishy!" squealed Darla as she reached out to grab him.

Gill flipped himself onto the tray beside Nemo.

"Tell your dad I said 'hi'," he said. Then Gill smacked his tail on a dental mirror, catapulting Nemo over Darla's waiting hands and into the spit sink. The little fish escaped down the drain!

Back in the harbour, Nigel dropped Dory and Marlin into the sea. Marlin was heartbroken. He thought that he had lost Nemo for good and swam off to be on his own.

Nemo soon met Dory. At first, she had no memory of who he was…. But when she finally did remember, Dory knew she had to reunite Nemo with his dad straight away!

Together, they swam after Marlin as fast as Nemo's little fins would let them.

There was a happy reunion between Marlin
and Nemo. Marlin finally realized that even
though Nemo was a little fish, he was
capable of doing very big things! They had
both learned that life was an adventure to
be lived to the full.

Meanwhile, the Tank Gang were
having an adventure of their own.
They had finally made their escape, but
now they just had to find a way to get
out of the bags!

Long ago, there was a kingdom called DunBroch nestled in the Scottish Highlands. Though the kingdom was young, the land was ancient – a place full of stories and magic … and danger.

Merida was the Princess of DunBroch. She lived for her rare days of freedom when she could roam the forests and hillsides of the kingdom with her beloved horse, Angus. She was a skilful archer, too, and practised endlessly.

Merida lived in the castle with her father and mother – King Fergus and Queen Elinor – and three younger brothers.

Elinor had high hopes for Merida and high standards for a princess. She thought a princess should be well-rounded, knowledgeable about her kingdom and above all, perfect in every way. In Queen Elinor's eyes, Merida had much to learn.

Even worse for Merida, her parents wanted her to marry a prince from a neighbouring clan.

"I'm not ready to marry!" Merida shouted.

But Merida's objection came too late and, before long, the ships of the neighbouring clans were pulling into DunBroch's harbour. The clans gathered in the Great Hall and the lords presented their eldest sons to Merida.

The princess was not impressed with what she saw. She sat at the front of the Great Hall, desperately trying to think of a way out of this marriage.

Then the queen announced that Merida would choose a competition for the lords' sons.

Sensing an opportunity, Merida declared excitedly, "I choose archery!"

The competition took place in the castle grounds. Merida watched from her throne as the lords' sons lined up before her.

But the sons were not very good archers, so when each had taken their shot, Merida leaped to her feet to take her turn.

"I am the first-born descendant of Clan DunBroch," she announced, "and I'll be shooting for my own hand!" Three times her arrows hit their marks and she was the winner!

Queen Elinor was furious with her daughter. "You don't know what you've done," she told Merida when they were back inside the castle. "It will be fire and sword if it's not set right." Merida did not understand that her victory could lead to war among the clans.

"You're a beast!" Merida replied. "I'll never be like you!" Angrily, she slashed the family tapestry between the images of her and her mother.

Sobbing, Merida ran out of the castle and rode Angus deep into the forest. Angus lurched to a sudden stop, sending Merida flying. When she got to her feet, she found she was standing inside a ring of giant stones.

A mysterious blue light flickered among the stones ... and then another ... until there was a whole chain of blue flames beckoning Merida towards a cottage.

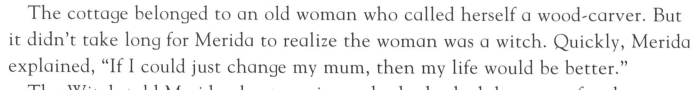

The cottage belonged to an old woman who called herself a wood-carver. But it didn't take long for Merida to realize the woman was a witch. Quickly, Merida explained, "If I could just change my mum, then my life would be better."

The Witch told Merida about a prince who had asked, long ago, for the strength of 10 men. Merida would get a similar spell.

The Witch set to work, slicing ingredients and throwing things into her cauldron.

When she was done, the Witch pulled out a cake and handed it to Merida. Within minutes, Merida and Angus found themselves back at the Ring of Stones. There was no sign of the Witch or her cottage!

Eagerly, Merida returned home. Her father was stalling the suitors by telling the tale of his battle with Mor'du, a fierce bear who had taken his leg. Merida found her mother … and gave her the cake.

But instead of changing Elinor's mind about the marriage, the cake changed
the queen into a bear!

"That scaffy witch gave me a gammy spell!" exclaimed Merida as the bear let
out an angry roar.

Merida helped Elinor-Bear sneak past Fergus and the impatient clans to
escape into the forest.

In the forest, Merida and Elinor-Bear found the Witch's cottage – with a riddle she'd left behind: "Fate be changed, look inside, mend the bond torn by pride." Soon a thick cloud enveloped them. When it cleared, the cottage was in ruins.

The next morning, Merida taught a hungry Elinor-Bear to fish and before long, Elinor-Bear was catching fish on her own. The two played together in the stream and for the first time in a long while, they enjoyed each other's company.

But Elinor-Bear was beginning to behave more and more like a real bear....

Merida looked everywhere for a way to help her mother. They came across the ruins of an ancient castle and Merida fell through a hole and into the old throne room. There was a tablet engraved with a picture of this kingdom's four princes. The tablet had been broken in two – the fourth prince was broken off from the rest.

"Split," Merida murmured. "Like the tapestry."

There were deep, angry claw marks all round the throne room – marks from the Witch's prince! With his great strength, he had become a bear – Mor'du! And he had destroyed the kingdom with his greed.

Elinor-Bear and Merida raced home and sneaked back into the castle.
Merida needed to repair the tapestry and 'mend the bond torn by pride'.
But first she faced the clans, who had begun fighting among themselves since
Merida left the castle.

Merida knew it was up to her to end the fighting. She marched into the centre
of the room. She was just about to agree to marry one of the lords' sons, when,
from the shadows, her mother stopped her.

Elinor-Bear mimed what she wanted Merida to say. "The queen feels … that
we should … find love in our own time," Merida translated.

The lords' sons agreed – they should all be free to follow their hearts!
Cheers rang out around the castle!

With the clans out of the way, Merida and her mother hurried upstairs to get the tapestry. But Elinor started acting more bear-like again!

Just then, Fergus entered and saw the bear.

"No!" Merida cried. "It's not what you think!"

Not recognizing his wife, the king locked Merida in the Tapestry Room to keep her safe. Then he and the other men chased Elinor like a wild bear!

Through the window in the Tapestry Room door, Merida saw three bear cubs in the hall. It was her brothers! They had eaten the remaining spell cake!

"Get the key!" she told them. The cubs chased the housekeeper, snatched the key and set Merida free!

Merida grabbed the tapestry, along with a needle and thread. Then she and her brothers climbed onto Angus and raced into the forest to save their mother. The king and the clansmen had chased Elinor-Bear out into the woods, hunting her down like a wild animal. As Angus ran, Merida mended the tapestry and the bear cubs steered.

Merida tracked Elinor-Bear to the Ring of Stones. But by the time she arrived, Fergus and the clans had already trapped her and bound her with ropes.

The king raised his sword to kill the bear when, from out of nowhere, Merida stepped in front of him.

"Are you out of your mind, lass?" Fergus exclaimed.

"I'll not let you kill my mother!" Merida told her father, protecting Elinor-Bear with her own sword.

Suddenly, another bear stepped into the ring.

"Mor'du!" Merida said with a terrified gasp.

The lords ran forwards to attack the giant bear. Mor'du swatted them away easily. Then he grabbed King Fergus and tossed him aside, too.

As Mor'du loomed over Merida, preparing to attack, Elinor-Bear broke free and charged. She and Mor'du fought a vicious battle but, eventually, Mor'du was defeated once and for all.

Merida threw the tapestry over her mother, the bear. For a while, nothing happened. Then Merida watched as the bear's eyes turned cold and black.

"I want you back! I just want you back, Mum," Merida said, throwing her arms round Elinor's neck. "I … I love you."

And finally, with dawn's new light, the spell broke. And mother and daughter knew that the bond between them was mended at last.

Young Carl Fredricksen gazed up at the movie screen in awe.
There, larger than life, was his idol, Charles Muntz,
the world-famous explorer.

The news story showed Muntz boarding his custom-made
airship, the *Spirit of Adventure*, accompanied by his trusty dogs.
They were off to South America to capture a creature known
as the 'Monster of Paradise Falls'.

When Carl grew up, he wanted to be an adventurer just
like Charles Muntz!

That afternoon, Carl met a girl named Ellie. She had turned an old house in their neighbourhood into a Charles Muntz-style clubhouse. Ellie invited Carl to be in her explorer's club. She fastened a badge made from a grape-soda bottle cap onto his shirt, saying, "You and me, we're in a club now."

From that moment on, Ellie and Carl were best friends. When Carl broke his arm, Ellie brought her adventure book over to cheer him up. Inside was a drawing she'd made of her clubhouse parked right next to Paradise Falls.

Ellie made Carl promise to take them to Paradise Falls one day.

When Carl and Ellie grew up, they got married.
They moved into their old clubhouse and fixed it up
to look just like Ellie's drawing. They didn't become
adventurers, though. Carl sold balloons from a cart and
Ellie took care of animals at the zoo. They were happy
together in their little house.

But they still dreamed of going to Paradise Falls.
They tried to save money for a trip to South America.
But they could never quite collect enough.

Many years went by and
Carl and Ellie grew older.
After Ellie passed away, Carl
continued to live in their
house. But he was lonely.
He missed Ellie.

Then one day, a boy named Russell knocked on Carl's door. Russell was a Junior Wilderness Explorer. He wanted to help Carl so that he could earn his Assisting the Elderly badge.

To get rid of Russell, Carl asked him to find a bird called a snipe. Russell headed off to look for it, not knowing that there was no snipe. Carl had made the whole thing up!

Not long after that, Carl received the bad news that he was being sent to live in a retirement home. But Carl didn't want to leave. All his memories of Ellie were in that house.

Remembering his old promise to Ellie, Carl came up with a plan. He tied thousands of balloons to his house and set sail for South America.

As the house flew over the city, someone knocked at the door. Carl was stunned. He was thousands of feet up in the air! Who could be knocking?

It was Russell! He had been under Carl's porch looking for the snipe when the house lifted into the sky. "Please let me in?" Russell begged.

Carl planned to let Russell get off in the next town, but he never got the chance. The house flew into a storm. In no time at all, they had landed in South America.

Carl was thrilled to discover they were just a few miles away from Paradise Falls. "We could float right over there!" he cried.

There was just one problem. They couldn't get back into the house – it was too high off the ground. But Russell had an idea: they could walk the house to the falls! They made a harness from the garden hose and set out for the falls, pulling the house behind them.

Along the way, Russell met an enormous bird. He named it Kevin. Kevin liked chocolate – he liked Russell, too.

But Carl didn't like Kevin. He tried to shoo it away, but it wouldn't leave.

Russell wanted to keep Kevin. As they set out for Paradise Falls again, he left a trail of chocolate for the bird to follow.

They hadn't gone far when they met a dog. "Hi there," said the dog.
"My name is Dug."

Carl and Russell couldn't believe it. The dog could talk!

"My master made me this collar so that I may talk,"
Dug explained, showing them the high-tech gadget.

Dug had been sent on a mission to find the bird.
He tried to capture Kevin, but the bird was too big. Kevin followed
Carl and Russell, so Dug followed them, too.

That night, they stopped to rest. Russell was worried. "Dug says he wants to take Kevin prisoner. We have to protect him!" he told Carl.

Carl saw how much Russell cared about Kevin. He agreed that the bird could come with them to the falls.

"Promise you won't leave Kevin? Cross your heart?" Russell asked Carl.

That last time Carl had crossed his heart was when he'd promised Ellie he'd take her to Paradise Falls. "Cross my heart," he finally agreed.

But the next morning, it turned out that Kevin was a mother. Her babies were waiting for her and she had to get back to them.

Kevin had not been gone long when three fierce dogs burst from the bushes. "Where is the bird?" snarled their leader, Alpha.

The dogs were part of Dug's pack. When they found out that he had lost the bird, they insisted on taking Carl and Russell back to their master.

The dogs led Carl and Russell to a huge cave. Inside, Carl got a surprise. The dogs' master was Charles Muntz, his childhood hero! Muntz had been in South America all these years.

The explorer invited Carl and Russell aboard his airship, the *Spirit of Adventure.*

On board the airship, Muntz told Carl
and Russell about his search for the Monster
of Paradise Falls. He wanted to be the first
person ever to capture the creature. As Muntz
talked, Carl realized the 'monster' was Kevin!
When Muntz found out that the bird had been
following Carl and Russell, he became angry.
He thought they were trying to steal it from him.

"Get them!" he told his dogs. Carl and Russell
ran from the airship. Suddenly, Kevin swooped
in. She picked up Carl and Russell. With Dug's
help, they escaped.

But Muntz tracked
them down in the
Spirit of Adventure.
"Get away from my
bird!" he ordered.
Then he set Carl's
house on fire!

Carl couldn't let his house go up in smoke. As he ran to beat out the flames, Russell was horrified. "You gave away Kevin!" he accused Carl.

Carl felt terrible, but he didn't know what to do. "I didn't ask for any of this," he told Russell. "Now, whether you assist me or not, I am going to Paradise Falls."

Carl towed the house the rest of the way to Paradise Falls on his own. He'd finally kept his promise to Ellie. But he still felt sad. He wished Ellie could have been on the adventure with him.

Inside the house, Carl found Ellie's adventure book. To his astonishment it was filled with photos of their life together. At the end was a message from Ellie. It read, 'Thanks for the adventure. Now go have a new one.'

Carl realized that Ellie had got her wish after all – their life together *had* been an adventure.

Suddenly, Carl heard a noise up on the roof. He rushed outside. Russell was rising into the air with a bunch of balloons.

"I'm gonna help Kevin even if you won't!" Russell called. He zoomed away, using a leaf blower to steer.

"No, Russell!" Carl cried. He tried to follow, but the house was too heavy. The balloons had lost too much air.

Carl made a decision. He'd kept his promise to Ellie – now he had to keep his promise to Russell, too. He pushed everything he owned out of the house until it rose into the sky.

153

Together, Dug and Carl set out to find Russell. Muntz had captured the boy and was holding him prisoner aboard the *Spirit of Adventure*. Using the garden hose like a rope, Carl swung over to the ship and rescued the boy.

Once Russell was inside the house, Carl and Dug went back for Kevin. Carl battled Muntz while Dug fought Alpha. Finally Carl, Dug and Kevin managed to escape onto the roof of the airship.

Russell steered the house close enough for his friends to climb inside. But then – **BANG!** Balloons popped and the house fell onto the top of the airship. When Carl toppled out, Muntz saw his chance. He raced into the house to get the bird.

Thinking quickly, Carl pulled out a chocolate bar from his pocket. "Russell! Hang on to Kevin!" he yelled. When Kevin saw the chocolate, she leaped through the window, taking Russell and Dug with her. They landed safely on the airship.

Muntz wasn't so lucky. As the house slid off the airship, his foot caught on a bunch of balloons and he drifted away.

Carl, Russell and Dug flew Kevin home in the *Spirit of Adventure*. Kevin was reunited with her babies. After a visit with the adorable chicks, it was time for Carl and Russell to go home, too. Muntz's dogs happily rode along with them. Dug was the new leader of their pack!

Not long after they arrived home, Carl proudly stood by Russell's side as the boy received his Assisting the Elderly badge. Now Russell was a Senior Wilderness Explorer! Carl smiled, knowing that he and his friend had many exciting adventures ahead.